Witch's Brew

Sapphire Lesbos

Every queer person looking for a bit of magic, or a home.

Chapter One

Dressing all in black and living in a tiny cottage made you look like one of three things: one, a witch; two, gay; three, emo. It really was unfortunate luck that Cynthia ended up as all three.

It wasn't her fault that people didn't like her for it either. She couldn't help the fact that she was a witch—she'd been born that way—or that she was gay—also born that way. Maybe she did play into the whole stereotype just a *little bit*, but it wasn't like it was all an act. She couldn't control the fact that her familiar was a black cat, and black hid stains easiest, and living somewhat situated amid a corn field surrounded by the woods was ideal because her magic worked best with plants and ravens happened to be excellent messengers.

Maybe it *was* a tiny bit ridiculous, but she loved it and wouldn't change it for anything. The only thing she didn't love were the comments.

They filtered through the air as she made her way through the field, rustling the corn on either side of her with her fingers. Black birds took off with cries all around as she moved along the maze, coming closer and closer until—

She burst out, surprising the children on the other side. Their stunned eyes remained wide for a moment before they burst into giggles, and she let her expression slide into an easy smile while she explained the rules of the corn maze. All the while, parents gave her odd, side eyed glances. Well, they could be like that. They still came to her farm. It might have been the only pumpkin patch around, but they *still* came, and that's what mattered.

They could be bigots so long as they paid her.

Stepping aside, Cynthia released the children and their grumbling parents into the corn maze, grinning silently to herself as she listened to their screams. Inevitably, they would ignore her rules, but so long as they were having fun . . .

She listened for a bit before giving herself a soft shake and making her way back toward the cottage for a short break.

The small, log cabin-esque building—single bedroom, just enough for herself and her cat—wasn't far from the large barn, so she took a quick detour. The barn's double doors sat open, as usual, with a collection of pumpkins piled up inside, along with stacks of hay bales and some wooden signs people could take pictures with. The usual tacky stuff.

She walked through, making sure everything on the counter was still shored up and safe, not that there was anyone around to mess with the register. On a random Monday in the middle of October, it wasn't as if she was especially busy, certainly not mid-day. There would be a whole herd of people later, inevitably, which was why she had workers scheduled to come in after four, but for now there was only the homeschooled kids and their grumpy parents.

Certain everything was good, as the kids would be occupied for a long while yet (unless they cheated, which was likely, she supposed, but frowned upon), Cynthia made her way to the cottage and let out a sigh, the cool interior washing over her in relief. Mid-October was still quite warm, and the dark clothes she wore did nothing to help that fact, even if her sleeves were long and loose and the fabric was light.

She passed a mirror, paused and did a double take, then retreated to stand in front of it to fix her dark hair. At some point during the tour, it had come loose and damn, she really did look like a witch right now, didn't she? Her once professional messy bun (could a messy bun be professional?) was loose, with ends sticking out all over the place, lopsided in one direction.

With a premade glamor spell spray, it was a quick fix, black nails glinting in the light from the window overhead as she sprayed it and felt the hair on her head adjust to her will. Running her hands down her front, she smoothed down the black dress. At least it wasn't stained.

"For some reason, today has been exhausting," Cynthia complained, giving her cat's head a rub as she passed him on her way into the kitchen. The black cat followed along at her heel, then hopped up on the counter beside the stove as she set the kettle on to boil. He bumped a mug as he did, knocking it off the edge. It jumped in the air before it could shatter against the ground, caught on invisible strands of magic she'd enacted a long while ago.

The cat had a tendency to knock things off the counter, though he denied he did it on purpose. Cynthia was skeptical of the statement, to say the least.

"Maybe because of the tiny gremlins running rampant on your farm," the cat said, voice low and guttural like a gnarled old man (though he hated the comparison), absently batting at one of the bunches of herbs that hung from the ceiling all around. They gave the room the most delicious smell, though they did crowd the space quite a bit. There was comfort in the plants, though, in knowing they had given their permission for her to use them in protection and other magic.

Cynthia shook her head. The kettle began to whistle. "It's not the gremlins so much as their parents."

"Ah, well, they have to get it from somewhere," Ruphys said, his green eyes finally abandoning the plant and turning to her. They were intelligent, even more so than most cats, though if you weren't looking closely you might not make out the cunning glint therein.

"I suppose that's true." Another scream came from outside and Cynthia sighed, letting her gaze fall to the window above the sink, overlooking the farm. Fields spread out along a relatively flat stretch of land, ending at the forest, a dark and foreboding shadow in the distance. For reasons she could not understand, some believed the forest to be haunted. She happened to find it delightful. "I should probably head back out there."

"Or you could hide in here and give me attention," Ruphys suggested, rubbing against her arm in emphasis.

A laugh barked from Cynthia's lips as she took up her cup of tea. "Don't tempt me. I have another field trip today after this one and I really don't feel like dealing with any more grumpy adults."

Nevermind that she could be considered a grumpy adult.

"Turn them into toads and let me play with them." Ruphys hopped down from the counter and followed behind as Cynthia moved toward her door once again, cup of tea now in hand. She made a mental note to not let herself forget this mug; there were far too many littered around the property. She was beginning to run out. Could she justify buying more?

"You know I can't do that."

"But think of how satisfying it would be." This time, the cat followed her outside, and she didn't stop him. If he wanted out, he'd find a way out, whether she shut him inside or not. He had enough magic in him to open the door or break a window if it struck his fancy, though he couldn't use much on his own. "And all you'd be doing is revealing their true nature."

Cynthia gave the cat a sharp look. "You'd better quiet down before anyone hears you."

He hopped up on a bale of hay and yawned. "I suppose you can't have me frightening anyone off."

"No, I can't."

"At least they don't do the whole pitchfork and bonfire thing anymore," the cat said, almost boredly. His voice sounded so human, so it was a bit odd when Cynthia looked over and found him licking his—

"I wouldn't put it past them," she said with a shudder. Maybe they wouldn't try to burn the witch out of her or whatever, but they could make it really hard for her to live here, and she wasn't eager to move again. Did no one understand how long it took to properly train ravens and raccoons? Or connect with the local fauna?

The shouts and screams of children grew closer as the first of them made it out of the corn maze and to the activities area out back, which drew a sigh to Cynthia's lips as she downed the last of her tea, at least as much as she could drink without downing the leaves. It was about time to wrap up the tour, wasn't it?

Though she didn't have much time, she swirled the grounds in the bottom of the tea cup and let them settle before giving them a cursory glance as she always did. Then did a double take. Second of the day. That couldn't be right, could it?

A heart sat at the bottom of the mug.

Love. If she was reading it right—and there was a possibility she wasn't—then the leaves predicted love for her at some point in the relative future. Which was crazy.

Well, it must just be the lavender leaves. It was such a finicky plant, so emotional. Better to do readings with proper tea, not herbal tea. Far more objective.

Leaving the mug behind on a bale of hay, Cynthia

took off down the lane to collect the children and their obnoxious parents and send them on their way with the nicest of niceties. Of course, no matter how rude they got with her, she could never respond in kind. She simply had to remind them that she was on a schedule, and they were on that same schedule by extension.

Stalks of corn seemed to reach out for her as she walked by, leaves bending in her direction. She scolded them with a cluck of her tongue and sent them back into place. They should've known better than to come after her when people were around. Of course, it wasn't exactly that they knew what they were doing; they weren't that conscious. They were plants after all. But they liked her, most plants did. Something about her magic drew them in, and she had to remind them to act like plants normally did.

It was similar with animals. Animals were often less obedient than plants, at least initially, but they were still drawn to her. Eager to do what she asked. And easy to understand as well. Most couldn't talk like Ruphys could, that was a talent that came with being a familiar, but she could still understand them. And they understood her.

All a part of their magic. Her magic.

She tilted her head and looked on at the gathered families with a barely suppressed groan. If only that magic extended toward humans.

Unfortunately, humans were a pain.

She clapped her hands together, summoning her most charming smile. Why couldn't that be a spell? "All right, everybody, are you ready to go?"

It took a bit of convincing, but she managed to get the children moving in the right direction, which was: to leave. Not quite fast enough, though, as the school bus pulled in as the first field trip was loading up.

She pushed down a sigh. Just make it through October and November, and she would be fine. She could go back to tending to her farm and stocking the tea shop and wouldn't have to deal with all of these children and their gremlin parents.

But this was the life she had chosen, and she wouldn't trade it.

Cynthia took a deep breath and readied a smile as the door to the bus opened—

And a woman with radiant skin and a shining smile stepped out, hair a blanket of bronze around her face, snatching the breath straight from Cynthia's lungs.

Chapter Two

As if made from a drop of sunlight, the woman shone, bronze skin glinting in the afternoon light, curls draping softly around her face. The yellow sweater she wore wasn't gaudy or draining, as it might have been on some, but lit her up all the more.

She stepped out of the bus in ankle high boots, the slit in the side of her light blue, daisy print skirt revealing the curve of her long, lithe legs.

Cynthia couldn't stop staring. She knew she needed to, knew the last thing she needed was to be condemned for perving on some—what was she? Parent? Teacher? If she was a parent, damn, she looked good.

The woman clasped her hands together, walking closer. Cynthia's mouth went dry. "Are you the owner, or is there someone else I need to talk to?"

Are you trying to catch flies with your mouth? Ruphys's voice sounded in her mind, and that alone made her snap her mouth shut. Stupid, stupid Cynthia. She couldn't start crushing on some random teacher/parent.

"Um, yes, yes, I'm the owner," Cynthia said quickly, snapping her eyes down and away from the woman. Get it together, focus. No drooling over customers. "Are you the, uh . . ." she trailed off. What had she intended to say?

"Yes, I'm the teacher," the woman said with a gracious smile. "Is there . . . something wrong?"

Cynthia looked back up, away from the gaggle of children making their way off the bus, parents with them. Whatever they were saying, she didn't make out, eyes locked on the teacher as her mind hurried to come up with some infinitely clever explanation.

It didn't work. "No, just, your outfit is amazing." Cynthia waved a hand at the skirt and sweater combination, internally cringing as she did. That was not the direction she should have gone. Nope, nope, nope.

"Really?" A shy smile broke out across her face as she looked down at her outfit, splaying out the skirt with her hands. "I was worried the yellow was too much."

"No, you really—really pull it off. Most people can't, but on you, it really shines."

The teacher looked back up, eyes crinkling as she stared at Cynthia. "Thank you."

A blush rose to Cynthia's cheeks unbidden. What was wrong with her? She'd been hiding on this farm for *way* too long. "But what would I know?" she rambled, throwing her hands down to her dress, wincing in her mind all the while. *Stop talking, stop talking, stop talking.* "I'm not really one for colors."

"I don't know," the teacher said, her look turning coy as her low voice rasped into Cynthia's ears. "I think you pull it off." She finished with a wink, and left Cynthia gasping for air as she turned back to her class, raising her voice as she called for order.

What just happened?

She recovered as fast as she could, catching her breath and wishing her glamor spell would clear the blush from her face, though unfortunately it didn't work that way. She followed the teacher over to the group, heartbeat rocketing when the teacher motioned for her to stand beside her, and put on her best *totally not panicking* smile for the class.

"Are you ready to listen to what—" she gave Cynthia a sidelong glance, and it took her a moment to realize the teacher was asking for her name.

"Cynthia," she supplied, blushing again as she avoided eye contact with anyone. Unfortunately, she couldn't avoid Ruphys's slightly amused attitude lingering in the backward space of her mind. Couldn't he just mind his own business?

"—Miss Cynthia has to say?"

"Yes, Miss Singh," the class said together, their little voices rising into a chorus. Cynthia raised an eyebrow. That was far more organized than many classes she got. Judging by the parents' faces, they were surprised as well.

"All right," Cynthia said, clapping her hands together. Right, this was something she knew how to do. Something she had a script for. Why couldn't she have a script for dealing with pretty girls? Something that involved more flirting and less panic-rambling. "If you'll follow me, we'll go ahead and get started . . ."

She turned on her heel and led away from the parking lot and toward the barn, where the tour began. Luckily, even with tours like these, they were mostly hands off once she explained the system and they left the barn. They might be more hands on than the crowds they got in the evenings, but it wasn't too bad.

Still, it was a relief when they began to make their way out of the barn toward the pumpkin patches. Now she could head inside, recoup for the night, bang her head against her wall for botching her conversation with the teacher so badly—

"You're really good with kids." She nearly jumped at the voice, spinning around to find that the teacher—Miss Singh—hadn't left with the rest. She stood off to the side with a slight upward tilt to her lips, leaning casually against a stack of hay.

"Er, thank you. I try." Cynthia winced. She really needed to go bang her head against the wall. "You're amazing with them, though. I mean, they jumped right to listen to you when you got off the bus."

She chuckled, lifted herself off the bales of hay, strode toward Cynthia. Cynthia's heart began a desperate attempt to escape her ribcage. "Don't let them fool you," she said. "They can be little shits sometimes."

A laugh burst from Cynthia's lips before she could stop it.

"I know," Miss Singh said, shaking her head, "I probably shouldn't be talking about them like that. But it's true!"

"I believe you!" Cynthia exclaimed, still giggling. She wasn't quite sure why it was so funny but she couldn't stop, little laughs bubbling up from her chest like fizz in champagne.

"I should probably be out there with them," the teacher said with a sigh, letting her head loll to one side and sending a cascade of soft waves over one shoulder. Her dark eyes flicked to Cynthia, catching her staring. "But you're far more interesting."

Heat filled her cheeks, and she knew she had to be turning the most excruciatingly embarrassing red. "I-I should hope so!" she stuttered out, looking away and waving a hand toward them. "After all, they're, like, five!"

"Most of them are eight and to be honest they can be quite interesting," the teacher said with a nod. "Though, none have their own pumpkin farm like you."

Cynthia looked down, cheeks warm. Was that all this was about? Her pumpkin farm? Of course it was, she was a pumpkin farmer after all—among other things—so why did she feel so disappointed?

"Would you like me to show it to you?" she asked.

The teacher grinned. "Sure!"

Cynthia nodded, swallowing the weird sick feeling in her stomach at the realization that all their talk had just been about business, and strode out of the barn. "You know, I never caught your name. Unless you want me to call you Miss Singh."

"Oh, no!" the teacher laughed. "It's Tabitha."

"Tabitha," she said, rolling the name over on her

tongue, then went warm all over again. "I'm-I'm Cynthia."

Tabitha gave a small, shining laugh and it lit up the world around them. "So you said."

Chapter Three

Cynthia tried her hardest to make the pumpkin patch and adjoining corn field sound interesting, though, to her credit, Tabitha looked nothing but interested.

"I can't believe you manage this all on your own, though!" Tabitha exclaimed, motioning around at the farm with both hands. She seemed to do that; talk with her hands. Throwing them this way and that with each point she made. Cynthia couldn't keep her eyes off them.

"I don't," Cynthia laughed, mind going to the many creatures who helped her maintain the farm. The ravens who helped her plant the cornfields in exchange for some of the corn she grew; raccoons who dug the holes for pumpkin seeds. Ruphys who—well, he wasn't always helpful. Elle and Taurin, who made it possible to open the farm up to outsiders.

"You don't?"

Cynthia blinked. Right, she couldn't exactly say anything about the ravens and raccoons and certainly not about the magical talking cat. Elle and Taurin were fair game, though. "No, I, uh, I have people who help me. Especially during the busy season. It's just me right now but come this evening, I'll have my team around because I can't handle all those people on my own."

Tabitha bobbed her head as she walked along. "That makes sense. What made you want to do this?"

"Huh?" She blinked again. No one had really asked her that before; usually questions were a lot more hostile, if they weren't self focused.

"What made you want to start and run a pumpkin farm?"

"I suppose I just felt called to it," Cynthia said with a shrug. It wasn't a lie, though it wasn't the whole truth, because she couldn't tell the whole truth. Yes, she was called to farming, only not purely out of passion, but because plants and animals responded to her due to the nature of her magic. Yes, she enjoyed her work, but she was also here because she'd been run out of the previous town she'd lived in, so it wasn't exactly entirely her choice. "What about you? What made you want to teach?"

"Well, partially because I had a degree I needed to do something with."

"So no particular passion for working with children?"

"Not at first, no," Tabitha said, looking over toward the pumpkin patch, where children roamed the hill with their parents and guardians, picking through the orange gourds. "But some things grow on you."

"They do, don't they?" Cynthia said, a small smile touching her lips as she looked around at her farm. Once, it seemed like a prison. A too small cottage and barren land she'd been bound to after her relocation. Now, it was home. And it had been home for a while.

When had that happened?

It came slowly, changing without anyone noticing, until it was so obvious it was staring her in the face and she wondered how she hadn't seen it before.

"I need a pumpkin," Tabitha announced, staring at the pumpkin patch as she placed her fists solidly on her hips, transforming into some sort of superhero before Cynthia's eyes.

"Well, your tour includes—"

"And I need you to help me," Tabitha said, talking over Cynthia as if she hadn't heard, snagging her hand and cutting her off. She began to march up the gentle slope toward the pumpkin patch, tugging Cynthia along behind her. And Cynthia was too shocked to do anything about it.

A cute girl was holding her hand. *A cute girl was holding her hand.*

"You-you need my help?" Cynthia stuttered out.

Tabitha turned to face her, smile flickering slightly, like a loose light bulb. Ready to go dark at any moment, at the wrong bump. "You're the farmer, I think you'd be able to help me pick out a good one."

"Of course!" Cynthia said quickly, getting the feeling she'd messed up somewhere and knowing she desperately did not want to mess this up. Maybe she shouldn't have been playing in it to begin with, but she was now, and she wasn't going to let her own disastrous nature destroy it just yet. "I'm sure I can help you find the perfect one."

"Oh, it doesn't have to be perfect," Tabitha said as she stepped off the dirt road and into the lanes of pumpkins. She looked back over her shoulder and grinned, and the sun over the hill behind her formed a halo around her head. Cynthia wanted to smack herself, it was so cute. "It just has to be unique."

Once again, for reasons she could not explain, Cynthia blushed.

She *really* needed to slam her head against the wall.

Despite the fact that she should probably be back at the barn getting things in order for the evening rush, Cynthia followed Tabitha into the pumpkin patch without protest, helping her search for the perfect—or most unique—pumpkin. She wasn't entirely sure what she was looking for; what constituted as unique, after all? But Tabitha made it fun, and Cynthia hadn't spent much time with anyone outside of work in a long time. She supposed this didn't count as outside of work, since she was technically working, but Tabitha wasn't one of her coworkers at least.

"What about this one?" Tabitha asked from a few rows ahead, rising with a small gourd in her hands. It was lumpy and sort of greenish and streaked with yellow. Cynthia winced; was that really what she grew?

Gourds were weird and all, but still . . .

Cynthia's eyebrows quirked downward. "I thought you wanted a pumpkin?"

"Well, that's true . . ." she said slowly, then set the gourd back down. She supposed that answered the question.

Cynthia continued looking. None of the pumpkins were especially unique. They were, well, pumpkins. They looked basically the same, especially with her magical influence.

Well, if she could make them uniform, what else could she do?

Cynthia bent down, as if inspecting something, then cast a quick look around. Everyone was looking elsewhere, even if a few eyes slid in her direction every so often, bringing judgment with them. Was it their clothes they had a problem with? Or were they simply wondering why she had followed them into the patch?

As soon as she was certain no one was looking at her, she cupped her hands around a pumpkin still attached to the vine and let out a small breath, willing her intentions into it.

Opening her eyes, she found in her hands a small white pumpkin with—an orange heart in the center?

Wow. How had she raced past intentions and straight into wishful thinking?

No matter. It was what it was now, and there was no changing it back. It was unfortunate, how once something changed, it could never be what it once was. Or maybe it was beautiful. Something like that.

She snapped the pumpkin from the vine and rose, turning to find Tabitha once again. "I think I found the one!"

Tabitha jumped at the sound of her voice, abandoning a rather large, bumpy pumpkin to walk over and inspect the pumpkin Cynthia presented.

At first, her expression was skeptical. It did look like a normal pumpkin from a distance, to be fair. But when she got close, her eyes went wide and her face lit up as if she'd just been presented with the whole world.

"Oh my god!" Tabitha exclaimed, reaching out then stopping short as if she didn't dare to touch the pumpkin. "That's incredible! Where did you find it?"

"Just there on the ground," Cynthia said, giving a short nod to the side.

"That's incredible," Tabitha breathed again, and this time, she took the pumpkin. And cradled it to her chest as if it was some sort of child. When she looked back at Cynthia, she winked. "I knew you'd be good."

For the third time in the past hour, Cynthia went entirely red.

She accompanied Tabitha the rest of the tour, uncertain what the protocol was in relation to pretty girls and pumpkin patches. If she was doing something wrong, it didn't show on Tabitha's face, though she didn't miss the laugh Tabitha failed to smother when Cynthia reluctantly admitted she didn't remember the way out of the corn maze. It's not like it was her fault; who expected her to memorize the route?

Shortly before four, half an hour later than Cynthia meant to wrap up the tour, she escorted the class and their lovely teacher back to the bus.

"Thank you for this," Tabitha said, clutching the pumpkin close as she spoke. "I fought for this tour, and you made it really special."

She made no effort to fight the smile off her face. "Of course. It was my pleasure."

"Is this what all your tours are like?" Tabitha asked, raising an eyebrow.

Cynthia blinked. What was the right answer? "Well, I try my best to make them nice, but this one was . . . special."

"I thought so," Tabitha said, her voice rich and low.

The low rumble of a car engine broke Cynthia's trance as she stared at Tabitha, trying to work out what to say next. "Uh, well, I'm glad you had a good time," she said as the little red pickup truck pulled into the gravel parking lot.

Tabitha nodded, beginning to shift her way over to the bus. Everyone else had already boarded.

She began to step into the bus and paused, looking over her shoulders and peering at Cynthia from beneath long, dark eyelashes. "Think I'll see you around?"

"Um, I don't know," Cynthia answered.

"You should," Tabitha responded with a twinkle in her eye. "I'm lots of fun."

Leaving Cynthia's mouth hanging open, Tabitha stepped up into the bus, door shutting behind her. She hardly had the sense to step backward as the school bus began to pull out.

Footsteps sounded as a slow crunch across the gravel parking lot as a young black man in a sweater vest made his way over.

"What was that?" Taurin asked, crossing his arms over his chest as he fell still beside the witch.

"I'm a disaster," Cynthia breathed out.

"What's new? And that really doesn't answer my question."

Chapter Four

"You know, that really isn't as bad as you think it is," Taurin said as he rang up someone's order at the counter in the barn. It was full, close to overflowing, which was why she was here and not out at the welcome tent greeting people. Working the second register to sell local goodies like bread and jam, alongside the pumpkins. "In fact, some people would consider it incredible for a cute girl to flirt with them."

"I know I would." Elle walked up behind them, squeezing past Cynthia to retrieve a drink from the fridge, the buckle on their overalls catching on the back of Cynthia's dress. Cynthia didn't have a moment's breath to tell them to get back to their counter. "I'm not sure what you're talking about, but I absolutely would not complain."

"A cute teacher flirted with Cynthia today." Taurin turned to explain, giving a sideways nod toward Cynthia.

Cynthia groaned. "See, that's the problem," she said, lowering her voice a bit. It was busy, the barn overflowing with noise, but she really wasn't in the mood to deal with any assholes tonight. "I don't know if she was flirting with me."

"She was flirting with you," Taurin said, as if he knew everything. He pushed up the sleeves of the white button up he wore under his sweater vest, speaking without looking at Cynthia or Elle, continuing to ring up people all while continuing a string of conversation. Cynthia had to make a conscious effort to pay attention to Taurin as she worked through customers.

"What did she do?" Elle asked, pausing between them. Nevermind the line of people over at the ice cream stand, they had to stand there and listen to gossip. Just like Ruphys . . .

Cynthia opened her mouth, but Taurin beat her to it. "She winked at her," he said meaningfully.

Elle gave Cynthia a long, significantly annoyed look. "She was flirting with you. What I wouldn't give . . ."

Shaking their head, strands of red-brown hair popping loose from the half bun atop their head, Elle walked back to their post. Thank the stars. That line was getting restless.

"You should flirt back," Taurin informed her.

"What?"

"You should flirt back. Did you?"

"Can we save this for later?" Cynthia requested. "When we're not slammed?"

"Sure." Taurin went back to work without complaint, and Cynthia let out a relieved breath. That was one less thing she had to worry about; he'd been unable to let it go since Cynthia admitted what had gone down with the teacher. Not that anything had, really. Maybe he'd forget about it by the time the day was done.

He did not forget about it by the end of the day. Apparently, Taurin didn't forget anything, and he didn't have anything better to do, because he cornered Cynthia as she counted the evening till.

And he brought it back up.

"So, tell me about this teacher girl," Elle said, leaning against the opposite side of the counter Cynthia stood behind. They could at least be sweeping or something, but like the cat Cynthia thought they'd get along with, they just stood there, blinking expectantly. Ruphys strode across the barn and hopped up beside them, purring when Elle began to scratch him behind the ears. Go figure, he wanted to hear too.

"There's nothing really to tell," Cynthia said, giving her head a slight shake. The bun she'd pulled her hair into was useless now, and she went ahead and pulled the rest of it down, letting her dark hair fall down to her elbows. It wasn't quite dark enough to blend in with her black dress.

"Bullshit," Taurin said, crossing his arms over the sweater vest he wore. "Spill."

Cynthia groaned, and glared at them both. Taurin was intensely interested, had been all day, but Elle didn't seem to care either way. Still, they didn't leave, and neither did he.

"The teacher from the field trip earlier was super cute," Cynthia said, spitting it out as quickly as I could. "I know I really shouldn't have, but I flirted with her a tiny bit—"

"Why shouldn't you have?" Elle asked. They paused scratching Ruphys behind the ear to look up at her. "I say you should always flirt with everyone but—" they shrugged "—that's just me."

"I shouldn't have because I don't have time for that and-and I just don't want to cause any sort of trouble."

"Only you would think romance is trouble," Taurin said, shaking his head.

"It's not that, it's just . . . I don't know. I just shouldn't have flirted with her—I mean, what if she took it badly?—and I have no idea if she flirted back. It's really not that big a deal, it's not like I'm ever going to run into her again, so we can just let it go."

"She wants you to run into her again, though," Taurin said.

"What?" Elle perked up, looking from Cynthia's unimpressed glower to Taurin's grinning face. "This I need to know."

Cynthia groaned and rolled her eyes. Taurin was making this a far bigger deal than it was. She should have never said anything.

"The teacher hinted that we should run into each other again."

Elle groaned. "You're an idiot!" they exclaimed, throwing both hands up toward her. "How can you think that's *not* flirting?"

"I—"

"What's her name?" they demanded.

"What?"

"What's her name?" Elle repeated, emphasizing each word. "Because I'm going to try to find her online so you can reach out to her. And if you don't, I will, because she sounds adorable."

Cynthia glared at them. "I don't need you to do that."

"Oh, but you clearly do," Elle said.

"Go home."

"Rude."

"Go home!" Cynthia began to laugh as she let out the words. "It's late. I'm tired! Get out of my hair."

"I'm going to get you a date," Elle said, walking toward the door.

"Leave me out of this!" Cynthia called back as they left the barn, yellow light glinting off their messy hair. When they walked out of view, Cynthia let her eyes slide to Taurin, glaring as he smirked. "I'll get you for this later."

"You'll thank me," he said.

"I'll get you for this," Cynthia repeated.

"See you tomorrow, Thia." His laugh echoed into the shadows of the night as he left the barn.

She slumped against the counter, unsure whether to laugh or cry. Were her friends wonderful or awful? She couldn't decide.

Ruphys made his way across the counter, deciding the register was the perfect place to sit. "So, are you done? I heard your head has a meeting with a wall."

Chapter Five

Cynthia did her best to forget about Tabitha. It didn't work.

The teacher continued to pop up into her mind and give her little gay thoughts, though she did her best to squash said gay thoughts into oblivion. She didn't want to deal with them right now. She just had to get through the season, then she could focus on whatever. Romance, herbs, tea, Christmas/Yule—whatever.

Except those little gay thoughts wouldn't leave her alone.

"Oh look," Ruphys said, boredom practically dripping from his tone. "There's another one. Let's see how you squash it this time."

Cynthia huffed and looked up at the cat. "Would you please stop watching my thoughts?"

"Why? It's like what you humans do. Counting sheep."

"You're counting my thoughts?"

"Your gay thoughts, specifically," Ruphys said as he stretched out, laying down across the side of the raised bed Cynthia worked over, his little black body stretched out in the sun. "I find them supremely amusing."

"Glad you're having fun," Cynthia muttered, and went back to going through her garden. A section of raised beds covered the stretch of yard behind her cottage, hidden behind fences and tall trees, carefully kept from general view. If anyone asked why, she would say it was to keep pests out of the herb beds. In truth, she never had any issue with pests, most animals were willing to listen to stay away in exchange for a bit of food. She simply didn't want people to question how she managed to grow herbs all year round.

From behind fences, no one could tell that she didn't have a greenhouse, but she'd never needed such things. In fact, she found they impeded the growing process. At least, she hadn't yet learned how to cooperate with them. Instead, she grew the herbs on natural magic all year round, no matter the cold or the heat. The plants just loved her that way, and the weather tended to be obliging.

Even as she snipped off stems and leaves for her harvest, they tilted in her direction, leaves brushing against her skin, vines reaching for her legs. A quiet rustle filled the garden, despite the lack of wind.

"Why do you squash these thoughts?"

"Huh?" Cynthia grunted. She finished harvesting the lavender before setting down the shears and looking at Ruphys. What was the cat talking about?

The cat rolled over and stretched in her direction, staring at her upside down. His green eyes reflected into her own. "Why do you squash these gay thoughts? You didn't used to, and I'm not sure what's different about them."

Cynthia opened her mouth, then shut it again sharply. What was different? "Because—" She shut her mouth again. "Because I just can't deal with that right now."

"But why not?" Ruphys asked. "I mean, you're always gay, aren't you?"

"Of course I am," Cynthia snorted. What sort of question was that? Ruphys should know better. He was there to witness her first moments of gay panic and her sexuality crisis, after all. He'd also been the first to tell her she was a lesbian.

"Then why is it a problem that you have these thoughts?" the familiar asked.

"Because . . ." Cynthia trailed off. What *was* the problem?

"But don't stop on my accord," Ruphys said. "I find it amusing to watch you chase them around in your mind and try to stomp on them."

She gave the cat a sharp glare and grabbed her basket, marching into the cottage to prepare the harvest for drop off.

She slammed the back door behind her, preventing Ruphys from following her immediately, and dropped the rounded basket on a low table with a thud. Sprigs of herb popped out and spilled across the wooden surface, making her double back after pausing in the doorway and letting out a splitting breath to gather them back up. The fresh herbs were only a small portion of her delivery to the tea shop, but she wouldn't let anything go to waste.

After organizing her harvest once again, Cynthia released a pent up breath and slumped into her palms against the table. Ruphys did have a point; these thoughts weren't any different than any in the past, and there was no reason to revert back to the scared little girl she'd once been, a girl who was too afraid to express herself or even acknowledge her own feelings. Even if that part of her did still exist. She could acknowledge that part of her and not feed it, at least not actively.

It did have a point, sometimes, though. At least, she felt like it did. She didn't want to have to relocate again, though she knew the Coven would be understanding. Even if starting over was an option, she didn't want to use it. She'd put her heart into building a space for herself, and she wouldn't give it up, even if that meant occasionally not listening to her heart.

It wasn't great at ideas anyway.

Flirting? Why did Cynthia think she was capable of it? She was too much of a disaster for such things.

The front door opened with a clatter.

"*Shit,*" Cynthia hissed, standing quickly. How long had she been sitting there? Was she late?

Elle strode through the doorway as if they owned the place, not waiting for a welcome or invitation inside, catching Cynthia with her hands tangled in her hair, attempting to tame the long raven locks.

"Catch you at a bad time, Cyn?" Elle asked, hardly giving Cynthia a second glance. They strode through the small foyer and stepped around the couch—it was so large it took up nearly the whole of the tiny living room—straight into the kitchen, out of view.

"I'd rather you not call me Cyn," Cynthia responded, tugging her hands from her hair and wincing slightly when hair caught around her nails.

"Why not?" Elle asked. The cottage was so small, it hardly distorted their voice at all. It also didn't hide the quiet thumping that indicated they were going through Cynthia's cabinets. What on earth were they looking for?

"Because it sounds too much like 'sin' and that just reminds me of . . ." She shivered, the chilling memory running down her spine and rendering her speechless.

"'Kay, got it," Elle said distractedly. "Why is everything you own organic? Can't a person just eat some junk shit?"

"Don't complain when I never gave you permission to go through my cabinets to begin with," Cynthia said. She picked up the basket and rounded the couch, forced to turn sideways to get past it without bumping into the wall.

Elle sat on the counter beside the sink, one ankle hooked over the other as they munched on a handful of nuts. "You need better food."

"You need to be out front," Cynthia fired back. It was the whole reason they were here, to man the farm and run today's field trips. Not to sit in her kitchen and eat all her food.

"Don't worry, I'll go," Elle promised, half garbled through a mouthful of food. "You just hadn't left yet and I thought that was odd."

"I'm running late," Cynthia said, giving her head a slight shake. Honestly, what was wrong with her? She was scatterbrained, having a crisis, and acting like her twelve year old self again . . . it was a mess.

She jumped to finish gathering up the last of the things she needed, a crate already filled with the dried herbs ready for the tea shop. Glass vials at the bottom for the shop to sell to customers, bags across the top for the shop to use. She set the basket on top of it and lifted it off the counter. "I'm leaving now."

"Be safe!" Elle called after her, lifting their voice into a sing-song. "Oh, wait!" Boots hit the ground, thudding loudly. "I found that girl for you! The teacher?"

Cynthia froze in the doorway. "What?"

"The teacher you told us about? I found her on Instagram for you!" The boots strode closer, but Cynthia refused to turn around. "You wanna know, don't you?"

I do.

"I have to go," Cynthia declared, and slammed the door shut after her.

The black pickup truck stuttered unhappily as Cynthia pulled up outside the tea shop and shut the engine off. Her eyes shuddered closed as she breathed out a relieved sigh; the truck had made it. Now to see if it would get her back home.

She opened the door and slammed it shut again, the whole vehicle seeming to rattle when she did. It was ancient and a bit rusted and dented in places and, honestly, it was a miracle the thing still ran. But until it broke down, she'd still drive it. Cynthia didn't want to have to get rid of her first car.

A car roaring down Main blared its horn as she hurried around to the bed of the old pickup. She spun around and flashed her middle finger, then quickly gathered up her supplies and hurried down the block toward the little tea shop.

Steeped Serenity was the single good thing about the rundown downtown stretch. Downtown was overly busy and had far too few places of note; everyone was angry, shops were either sketchy, gross, overpriced, or part of a franchise, and the whole place was cramped and devoid of meaningful plant and animal life. A hostile environment. But *Steeped Serenity* . . .

As its name implied, it was a slice of serenity, something the town desperately needed. It was also the only place Cynthia ever bothered visiting, and enjoyed.

The door jingled as she stepped inside and froze in the doorway, letting out a contented breath. The incredible, refreshing scent of brewing mint and steeped lavender filled her nose and washed over her like a cold shower, lending a new sense of energy to her.

Mmm, tea.

This was the best part about tea. It wasn't simply energizing, like coffee was, and it certainly wasn't anxiety inducing like coffee. It was soothing. Energizing. Refreshing. There was so much variety and it always smelled amazing.

"Cynthia!"

She looked over the top of her basket and grinned. "Nora! How are you?"

"Doing incredible," the older woman behind the counter said with a genuine smile. "What can I get you?"

"Oh, I don't know, whatever you think is best?" She knew, no matter what, she could trust Nora to brew up something incredible. Maybe it was simply her magical power—don't tell, but she's a witch too—but more likely it was the years of research she'd put into the craft of tea brewing. And yes, it was a craft. No, it wasn't just dropping a tea bag into some boiling water.

Nora busied herself behind the counter as Cynthia strode across the unusually empty dining room. It was a cozy place, with twinkling fairy lights on the walls, a book nook with comfortable chairs in one corner, and a desk counter along one wall with high stools beneath it where college age students often worked on computers. A large tree grew from a pot on the floor in the corner where the register counter met the wall, broad leaves reaching up to lay atop the wooden countertop. Hanging pots hung from the ceiling near the broad storefront windows, cuttings from Cynthia's garden growing in them.

Cynthia deposited the crate and basket on a table

near the front counter and doubled back, giving each of her little sprouts a bit of love. They perked up when they saw her, spinning toward her fingers with more love than her cat had ever given her. Damn stingy creature.

"Careful, 'Thia," Nora called. A kettle began to whistle. "You don't want to draw attention."

"You don't have to remind me," Cynthia said quietly. Nora meant well, but she didn't have to act like Cynthia didn't know what she was doing. She wasn't an idiot, she'd been relocated before, knew how awful it was, and knew to be careful not to get outed. Giving her plants a bit of love while the shop was empty wasn't going to get her in trouble, even if it made her look like a weirdo who liked petting plants.

"Tea's about ready," Nora said. "What did you bring for me today?"

Cynthia turned as Nora stepped out from behind the counter, drying her hands on the old fashioned, embroidered apron she wore.

"I brought you a good restock of everything, but my mint's really out of control so there's quite a bit more of that than anything else," Cynthia explained as she joined Nora over the basket and crate. Nora was up to her elbows in herbs, some dried, others fresh, all smelling incredible.

"Mint is a bit wild," Nora agreed. "How have you been?"

"All right," Cynthia said with a shrug. "Nothing's really changed, I guess."

Nora turned, following Cynthia as she strode to the counter to retrieve her tea. "Then why do you seem off?"

"Are you reading my emotions?" Cynthia accused, giving her a sharp look. Nora should know better.

Nora laughed. "No, but your vibes are affecting the whole shop. What's up?"

Cynthia stared at her, wishing she could hold back, then let out a sigh and relented. There was no point in holding out. "I've just been stressed with work. And there's this girl."

Nora laughed again, and Cynthia glared. "Of course. A girl. Did you break up?"

"What? No!" Cynthia exclaimed. "I'm not dating anyone."

"Oh, so that's the problem."

"No, it's not. I don't want to date anyone."

"Then being single shouldn't be an issue."

"No—" She groaned. Nora just wasn't getting it. "I mean, there's this girl, this teacher, who flirted with me the other day and—"

"And you can't get her out of your head," Nora said, nodding sagely. Her gray speckled brown hair bobbed around her shoulders.

"You're reading my emotions."

"I'm sorry!" Nora exclaimed, in a not entirely sorry way. "It's so hard not to. They're written all over your face! And they're stinking up my shop."

"Sorry." Cynthia threw up her hands in defeat. "I just can't get her out of my head! She was so cute and I think she flirted with me, which is my fault because I flirted first but I really shouldn't have—"

"Why not?" Nora asked. "You only live once, dear."

"Because I don't want to stir up trouble."

"And love is trouble."

"Who said anything about love?"

"I did, keep up."

Cynthia chuckled, shaking her head. Nora lightly swatted the back of her head as she stepped around her, before continuing on with conversation.

"I know you're cautious, 'Thia, and that's good, but you also need to be able to live a little," she said. "That's why the Coven put you here. So you'd have a safe place to live, out of hiding."

A rattling sigh shook forth, and Cynthia sipped at her still too hot tea before answering. "I just don't want to mess anything up."

"'Thia, dear, you're not going to mess anything up by living a little, at least not any more than anyone else messes things up by living," Nora said. "Trust me. I've been around a while. You can't just hide and try to make sure nothing bad ever happens."

Cynthia groaned. "I hate that you're right. And that my cat agrees with you."

"Ruphys is wise," Nora said, then chuckled. "When he wants to be." She sat down in a chair across from Cynthia, the wrinkles on her cheeks increasing when she smiled. "Now tell me about this girl."

Though she tried to resist, a smile broke through.

"She—"

The door jingled and Cynthia cut off quickly to look toward the door, mouth falling open when Tabitha stepped inside.

Chapter Six

Sunshine shone in a halo behind the teacher, turning her brown skin to bronze. The door behind her shut and the light faded off just as her eyes fell to Cynthia.

Cynthia snapped her mouth shut. No, she was not about to look like an idiot in front of Tabitha again. Not if she could help it.

Tabitha blinked in surprise, but quickly recovered, full brown lips splitting into a brilliant smile. "Oh, hi. Fancy seeing you here."

"Hi," Cynthia said, her response stiff. *No, that sounded awkward.* "What are you doing here?" *Shit, that was more awkward.*

"It's the best place around to get tea," Tabitha said, making her way toward the desk as Nora squeezed around Cynthia with a knowing smirk.

"Um, yes." Cynthia quickly stood, sloshing tea over her hand as she did. She winced, and set the cup down. "Yes." She was botching this, wasn't she? "It really is the best."

"I've also heard a local farmer supplied a lot of the herbs used here," Tabitha said. She stopped a few feet from the counter, parallel to Cynthia, and looked over with a coy grin. "That wouldn't be you, would it?"

"It-it would," Cynthia stuttered as her cheeks went warm.

Tabitha moved in, closer and closer until Cynthia lost the ability to breathe. When she spoke, warm breath brushed Cynthia's cheek. "I was hoping it was you."

Tabitha's rasping voice went straight to Cynthia's core, words leaving her stomach fluttery and warm.

She shifted quickly, trying to ease the weight and warmth in her middle, all the while locked in place by Tabitha's intent gaze.

Nora cleared her throat, catching Tabitha's attention and saving Cynthia from it. Knees weak, she dropped back into her chair and sipped her tea, barely able to hear as Nora took Tabitha's order and exchanged small talk.

What the hell is wrong with me?

The slamming in her chest slowed to a reasonable rate after a few moments, only for it to skyrocket once more when the chair across from her scooted outward and was quickly occupied not by the tea shop owner, but by Tabitha.

"Hi," Tabitha said, and this time her voice wasn't deep or sultry, it was soft and sweet like lavender and honey.

"Hi," Cynthia responded, barely able to lift her voice over a murmur. What was wrong with her? It wasn't like Tabitha was the first pretty girl she'd ever seen . . .

though, she was the first one to really flirt with her in a while. Had she forgotten how to flirt?

Well, that would imply she knew how to flirt in the first place.

Cynthia opened her mouth to say more, then shut it, tongue refusing to come up with a better response for the girl. And neither Tabitha nor Nora saved her. Silence stretched until it became a near tangible thing, a wall between them she could reach out and touch, and it wouldn't budge.

Nora walked over and set a steaming mug of tea in front of Tabitha, but instead of staying to talk, she walked away. And hid. In the storeroom. Leaving Cynthia to face Tabitha alone. *Why?*

After blowing at the top of her mug for a long moment, Tabitha set the mug back down and looked across the table at Cynthia, catching her before she could drop her eyes again.

"You don't have to talk to me if I'm making you uncomfortable," she said softly, reaching toward her with one hand, brown fingers stopping just before they touched Cynthia's pale arm.

"No, no!" Cynthia explained, and frantically shook her head. This was going wrong, how could she stop it? "It's not that, I promise. I want to talk to you. I'm just . . . bad with words."

Her expression morphed into a sheepish smile, hoping the explanation was enough not to run her off.

"Really?" Tabitha asked. "You seemed pretty good

at the farm . . ."

"That's because I had a script!" Cynthia explained. "I knew what to say then, and it still didn't go exactly how I wanted. But now you're sitting in front of me and I don't have a script and you're so pretty you kinda just fry my brain and oh my god, I really should shut my mouth."

Heat flooding her face, Cynthia buried her head in her hands, wishing she could be anywhere but here. Why couldn't she just talk like a normal person?

Only when Tabitha began quietly laughing did she dare peak through her fingers. "What's so funny?"

"Nothing," Tabitha said, shaking her head. "It's just cute. And I'm really glad to know I didn't scare you off."

"Same," Cynthia said. "I really thought I'd scared you off."

"By being a little awkward?"

"By being . . . me." She motioned at herself, at the signature black dress with wide sleeves, curling silver rings on her fingers, her long raven tresses. "It usually works."

"Does that mean you want to scare people off?" Tabitha asked, leaning onto the table and plopping her head onto her hand. Curiosity made her eyes gleam, a hint of a smile on her lips.

"Sometimes?" Cynthia admitted.

Tabitha giggled. "I kinda like that."

Cheeks growing warm, Cynthia grinned. "Really?"

"Yeah," Tabitha said, the corners of her eyes crinkling. Then she looked down sharply, drawing her fingers tight around the mug and taking a long sip. "This tea is really good too."

"What did you get?" Cynthia asked. The type of tea a person enjoyed could say a lot.

"Um, I'm not sure," Tabitha said, setting the cup of tea down. "I'm not really a tea drinker."

"No?"

"Um, no." Tabitha let out a small chuckle.

"What made you so interested all of a sudden?"

"You," Tabitha said, her eyes flicking up then quickly back down at the cup. "I come in here occasionally but not often, until I learned you were involved with it."

"Oh." Her stomach fluttered. She hadn't considered Tabitha might seek out the tea shop because of her.

"So how are you involved?" Tabitha asked.

"I supply the herbs Nora used," Cynthia said. "And Nora is an . . . an old friend." Yeah, that was as good a way as any to describe who Nora was to her. Friend, teacher, family, any of them could have worked.

"So I take it you like tea?"

Cynthia lit up. "I love tea! There's so much variety, so no matter what your taste is, you can probably find something you like, and it's so much better for you than coffee. And there are other uses too! Like chamomile being calming. And raspberry leaf tea is good for period cramps!"

"Really?" Tabitha asked. "I didn't know that."

"Tea is good for a lot of things," Cynthia said with a nod. "I mean, you have to be careful to do your research about what you're drinking so you don't hurt yourself, but in general, it's great. Even just for something to sip on while you work."

"That's amazing," Tabitha said. "I'm usually more of a coffee girl but I'm thinking I might have to let you corrupt me."

"You—" Cynthia swallowed hard, trying to convince herself to keep going. "You should let me."

"What's your favorite?" Tabitha asked as she swirled her cup in one hand before taking a sip. "What would you recommend?"

"I absolutely love chamomile and lavender tea," Cynthia said. "It's so calming and soothing."

Tabitha nodded along. "You should make it for me sometime."

"I should—what?"

"You should make it for me sometime," Tabitha repeated, and took a smooth sip of her tea.

"I, uh, yeah. Okay," Cynthia stuttered. "I could do that."

A smile snuck onto Tabitha's face as she finished sipping at her tea.

"I—" The blaring alarm on her phone went off and Cynthia nearly tumbled out of her seat as she went for it. Late. She was going to be late again. "Shit. I have to get back to the farm."

Tabitha set her cup down sharply. "Do you have to?"

"Yes." Cynthia winced. "I'm sorry. I promised Elle and Taurin I'd be back in time to run the front gate at the farm, and I think I'm already going to be late."

"Oh," Tabitha said. She slumped before picking herself back up again, pasting a smile back onto her face. "So we'll do tea another time?"

"Yes!" Cynthia winced again. That was too eager, wasn't it? "Yes, I would love to. Just not tonight." She shut her phone off and hurried toward the door.

"I'm looking forward to it!" Tabitha called out as Cynthia rushed out the door, hurrying for her car.

She rushed to the black pickup and pulled open the door, jumping in the front seat. Then slumped and groaned into the steering wheel. What had she just agreed to?

Chapter Seven

By the time Cynthia made it back to the farm, the rush had already hit. She hurried to find a parking spot, forced to park far further away than she would have liked, then hiked to the barn, coming to deeply regret her heeled boots.

"You're late!" Elle shouted as Cynthia hurried into the barn, sticky with sweat, long pieces of hair plastered to the side of her face. "What happened?"

"Sorry, sorry," Cynthia said, hurrying behind the counter. There was no time to fix herself up first, the barn was overflowing. Maybe if she could help get this under control, she'd be able to get to the front gate.

"I thought you just had to drop things off at the tea shop," Elle said. They stood behind the main counter, the ice cream counter closed, with Taurin at the main gate. He was stuck, so Cynthia decided to head to the barn rather than attempt to extract him. She'd apologize later, and replace him as soon as possible.

"I know, I'm sorry!" Cynthia exclaimed. "But I ran into Tabitha."

"Really?" Elle exclaimed. Their outrage

immediately transformed to surprise. "Where?"

"The tea shop. She came in to try and find me."

"Really?" Elle squealed. "How did it go? Please tell me you didn't botch it. If you botched it, I'm quitting right now."

Cynthia glared at them. "I didn't botch it. And you wouldn't quit."

"I might."

"You'd be back tomorrow."

"Only if you stock your kitchen better."

"I think Tabitha asked me on a date," Cynthia admitted.

Elle's eyes went wide. "Really?"

"Or, well, she made me ask her on a date? Kinda? I'm not sure."

"Thank the stars, you didn't botch it," Elle breathed out, throwing up their hands overdramatically. "When are you going out?"

"I'm not sure," Cynthia admitted. "I didn't really get that far."

Elle dropped their hands down onto the counter. "You botched it. I'm done. I'm done!" They shook their head and began to walk away.

"Hey, no, Elle! Come back!" Cynthia called.

Elle planted their hands on their hips, glared at Cynthia for a minute, then came marching back. A patchwork skirt kicked out around their feet as they stomped deliberately in heavy boots. "Fine. But I'm giving you her Instagram handle at the end of the night and you're going to take it."

"Okay," Cynthia conceded. "Just help me. Please."

"You're also getting better snacks."

"Deal! Now are you going to help me?"

Elle shrugged. "Sure. I've got what I wanted."

Chapter Eight

Tabitha's Instagram page stared up from her phone, and Cynthia's heart slammed as her finger lingered over the blue *follow* button. Why was this so hard?

Just follow her. Press the little blue button and then maybe start a conversation.

Cynthia's finger didn't move.

This was far harder than it should have been.

"How long are you going to stare at her page?" Ruphys asked, stepping from the back of the couch onto her shoulder to peer over it. He stepped on her hair, tugging it down and making her wince, but in his usual fashion, didn't care a bit.

Cynthia rolled her eyes and shut the device off, dropping it into her lap. Ruphys hopped off Cynthia's shoulder and landed beside her, curling up contentedly on a pillow.

"Do you think this is a bad idea?"

Ruphys flicked his ears forward. "What do you mean?"

"Do you think talking with this girl—Tabitha—is a bad idea?" Cynthia asked, tightening her fingers together as she asked the question.

"What do you mean?" Ruphys asked, and for once he actually seemed serious. Which meant Cynthia was in deeper than she thought.

"I mean, I don't want to mess things up again," Cynthia admitted, wringing her hands together until they formed a knot. She didn't want to leave again. She'd gotten settled, built a life, made friends, even if most of her friends were technically coworkers. Or more technically employees, but she didn't like to think about them in that way. "I know Nora said that I shouldn't be afraid of that, but how can I not?"

"I understand," Ruphys said quietly. He fell silent, tail flicking back and forth in thought. Cynthia waited, gnawing at her lip while Ruphys prepared his response. Finally, Ruphys lifted his head, strikingly intelligent green eyes meeting Cynthia's own. "But tell me, because I cannot figure it out: Why would this mess things up?"

She bit down on her lip then released it. "I'm not sure," she murmured. "But what if it does?"

"Then your anxiety proves you right," Ruphys said. "But until then? You're being irrational. And for what it's worth, I don't think anything bad is going to happen if you talk to this teacher a bit."

"Yeah?"

"So long as she doesn't have a dog," Ruphys stated, and began to knead his paws into the pillow, no longer paying attention to Cynthia.

"What?" she laughed.

"If she has a dog, I'm filing for divorce."

"You can't divorce me, we're not married. You're a part of me." She tapped her head, grinning at the cat.

Ruphys gave her a sideways look before turning away primly. "The logical part of you, clearly. No sane person would want a dog."

The amusement building in her chest burst and Cynthia began to laugh, giggling harder and doubling over when Ruphys gave her an afronted look.

"Never change, Ruphys, never change."

The quiet night ate in on Cynthia, only her too-bright phone screen lighting up the small room in the dark. Her heart beat too fast; chamomile-lavender tea had done nothing to calm it. Tabitha's page continued to stare back at her. Ruphys said it wouldn't mess things up. Nora said it wouldn't mess things up. And yet Cynthia still couldn't shake the horrible fear that it would.

But . . . why not listen to the two people she trusted most in her life? They cared for her, wanted what was best for her. They wouldn't steer her wrong.

She sucked in a deep breath. She didn't want to live in hiding. She made the decision not to years ago.

She tapped the follow button. All right, no taking that back now. She wouldn't hide from whatever was possible with Tabitha, at least not fully. Even if she wouldn't ever be able to be open with her about who she was.

Cynthia groaned, turning her phone off and dropping her head back onto the pillow in the dark. Why was being a witch so complicated?

<h1 style="text-align:center">Chapter Nine</h1>

These were the nights Cynthia loved best. The moon shone above, though the sky was still a hazy blue, clear of clouds. The scent of rain still clung to the air from the earlier shower, cooling down the mid autumn heat and leaving everything slightly sticky but it didn't matter because it felt good. Red and orange leaves clung to their trees in picture perfect shades, at the peak of their transformation. There was something poetic about being the most beautiful when dying.

It wasn't that it was more beautiful because it was dying, it was that you savored it because you knew it wouldn't last.

People filled the farm, but it wasn't as crazy as it could be. There was something lethargic about an evening after rain. It was nice, a good change of pace.

For once, Cynthia didn't have to be everywhere at once. And when her phone buzzed in her back pocket, she could actually answer it.

Her heart fluttered when Tabitha's name appeared on the screen, over a wallpaper that was a photo of her latest tarot card drawing. A reminder to herself to remain grounded and calm.

But that damn heartbeat. It had been happening more and more over the past week, and she didn't really mind.

She keyed in her password to read Tabitha's latest message.

Tabitha: I swear, we need a break before Halloween more than we do before Thanksgiving

Tabitha: these gremlins are getting awfully full of themselves

The grin on Cynthia's face grew wider. Somehow, even just talking about little things like this lit her ablaze. Tabitha was a person just like everyone else, and talking to her could be as easy as speaking to Taurin or Elle. Except there was a tea date looming over Cynthia's head. She still hadn't managed to bring that one up yet. Thankfully, Tabitha didn't press it.

Cynthia: aww, what are they doing now?

Cynthia: don't throw any out a window ⚫

Tabitha responded almost immediately.

Tabitha: I'll try ⚫ they make it difficult

Tabitha: even thinking about them is driving me crazy rn

Cynthia: yknow, I have a tea for that

She cringed as soon as she sent the message. Why did she do that? Would that mean she'd have to invite Tabitha over for tea? She wasn't ready for that. She was still too busy, had too much to do, and didn't have the time for a date.

Tabitha: is that an invitation? ;)

Cynthia shut her phone off and stuck it in her pocket. Guilt immediately flushed to her face, leaving a sour taste in her mouth. What was she doing? *Just respond, just respond and ask her out, invite her over for tea . . .*

But that was scary. What did you even do on a date? What did you talk about?

She didn't know, and she wasn't ready to find out or flounder her way through one.

Taurin's shoulder bumped against hers and Cynthia nearly leapt out of her skin. She blinked rapidly, heartbeat slowing as she took in a deep breath. Why was she so jumpy?

"What's up?" Taurin asked. "You seem off."

"I'm fine."

"It's that girl of yours, isn't it?"

"I don't have a girl," Cynthia scoffed.

"No, but you like one," Taurin said. He bumped into her arm again. "What's up with her?"

Cynthia crossed her arms over her chest. "She wants me to ask her on a date."

"Oooh, really?" Taurin's face lit up. "Spill. I want details."

"I just told them. She wants me to ask her on a date."

"Oh." His eyebrows twisted into a frown. "So why don't you?"

Cynthia sighed.

"Oh, don't tell me you're scared?" Taurin groaned. "Don't you want to go out with her?"

"Yes, but—" She groaned again. "I don't want to mess things up."

"Ask her out."

"Taurin—"

"Ask her out!" he exclaimed, throwing up his hands in exasperation. "I'm serious. Just do it. Or you're going to drive her away."

Cynthia sucked in a deep breath. He was probably right. "I'll do it."

"Now?"

"No, not now!" she exclaimed, crossing her arms tightly over her chest. "I'm working."

Taurin snorted and shook his head. "Sure. Whatever you need to tell yourself."

What did he want from her? "I—"

He held up his hands, backing away. "No, you do what you need to. I clearly don't know anything."

Cynthia huffed as he walked away. What did he care? It wasn't like this affected him at all. Why was he so invested?

She let up a pent up breath and glanced down at her phone. Nothing. Great, she really was going to drive Tabitha off, and she wasn't sure how to stop it.

What was she going to do?

A finger jammed into her back. Cynthia jumped, spinning around toward the person behind her, and her mouth fell open.

Tabitha stood behind her, crossing sweater clad arms over her chest, face twisted into a grumpy frown lit by the electric torches surrounding the farm. "You ghosted me," she said, lips drooping into a pout.

"No-No!" Cynthia exclaimed. No, this isn't what she wanted. She didn't want to make Tabitha mad, or drive her off, or scare her away . . . "No, I've-I've just been busy."

Tabitha raised an eyebrow, looking around at the farm. It was far from busy. The parking lot was half empty. No one stood in line in the barn. "Busy?"

Cynthia winced. She opened her mouth to speak, but Tabitha beat her to it.

"Look, if you don't want to go out with me, I get it. Just tell me. We could be friends." Her expression went soft, imploring. "Just be honest with me, Cynthia."

She let out a long, shaking breath. "I . . . I don't just want to be friends with you," she said, eyes darting down to the hem of Tabitha's linen skirt and the combat boots she wore. "I-I like you. But I . . ."

"You what?" Tabitha prompted, her voice gentle. The sort of voice a teacher would use with a struggling student. Cynthia didn't know whether to love it or hate it.

"I don't know how to ask you out." She spat out the words and immediately sucked in a breath, eyes darting up at the last moment to catch Tabitha's reaction.

She softened, and let out a small laugh. "Really? That's it?"

Cynthia's ears went warm. It was ridiculous. Why was she ridiculous? She was going to scare her away. "Sorry."

Tabitha leaned in, voice dropping to a reverent whisper. "Would it be easier if I asked you out?"

A gasp of relief burst from Cynthia's lips. "Yes please," she breathed, not caring if Tabitha thought she sounded desperate. She hadn't scared her off. She wasn't angry. Thank the stars.

Tabitha smiled, warmth shining from her cheeks. "Okay, I can do that." She glanced around before her chin dipped, almost shy. "Cynthia, would you like to go out with me?"

She nodded, warmth rushing to her head in a roar, giddy as she smiled. "Yes!"

"How about . . . When are you free?" she asked, tilting her head to the side.

"Tomorrow!" Elle popped up from somewhere behind her, Ruphys in their arms. "She's free tomorrow evening!"

"What?" Cynthia blinked, not sure how to react first. How long had Elle been listening in? What did they mean, Cynthia was free tomorrow evening? The farm was open, she had to be there—

"Yes," Taurin agreed, coming out of nowhere. Had he been listening in too? "You're free tomorrow. We'll cover it. Go on your date, please."

Tabitha giggled. "Seems like it's settled, then. I'll see you tomorrow?"

Her annoyance vanished, replaced by a smile she had to force through to talk. "See you tomorrow."

Chapter Ten

"I can't do this."

"Yes, you can," Taurin said. He squeezed Cynthia's shoulders from behind, expression reassuring in the mirror she stared into.

"What am I going to wear?" she moaned.

"Do you ever wear anything but black?" Elle asked from Cynthia's bed. Why they had decided Cynthia's bed was the perfect place to sit, Cynthia had no idea. "Like, I would bet five dollars you only have black clothes in your closet."

"Only five?" Taurin asked, incredulous as he swung around to face them.

"It's a versatile color, okay?" Cynthia said. "It's hard to get dirty. Doesn't stain. It's *smart*."

"Whatever you say," Elle said, rolling their eyes as they spoke. Cynthia glowered, crossing her arms over her chest. It wasn't like it was a bad thing she wore black. And she *did* own more than just black. She had . . . gray, at least. Wasn't there some purple in there?

"Oh!" Cynthia's eyes lit up and she jumped forward, pushing into the packed closet. She came back out gasping for air, gripping a hanger tightly in her hand. From it hung a gorgeous velvet dress in royal purple, with a full, pleated skirt built to hug the waist and hang lower in the back like a train. The sleeves were bell style, her favorite, and golden lace trim along the hemlines and waist.

Elle wolf whistled.

"Now *that* is a first date dress," Taurin said, taking it from her hands to admire it. He ran his fingers down the skirt, smile blooming. "Oh, it's gorgeous. Where did you get this and why on earth were you hiding it?"

Cynthia blushed. "I got it for a special occasion," she said, thinking back to the witch's gala, an event she'd only attended once. "And it's entirely impractical to wear it! Also, I forgot I had it."

"How do you forget something like that? If I wore dresses, that's what I'd wear," Elle said, crawling across the bed to touch it. Taurin held it out to them, and when they ran their fingers down it, they gave an appreciative nod.

"Agreed," Taurin said, before handing the dress back to Cynthia. "Now, go put that on and get ready for your date."

Cynthia clutched the dress to her chest, attempting to resist the giddiness rising within her. "Are you sure you two will be fine tonight?"

"Of course."

"Without a doubt."

"Do not even think about coming back."

"If you do, I'll steal your cat."

Cynthia turned to glare at Elle. "Do try."

Elle put on a prideful grin and leaned over to scratch Ruphys between the ears. "I'm pretty sure he likes me better."

He might, Cynthia thought, *but only because he likes your bullshit.*

"All right," Cynthia said, more to herself than to her friends. She was going on a date tonight. Well, not going anywhere, but she did have a date tonight. And it was going to go well. Yes, it was going to go well. "All right. I'm going to go get ready. Thank you so much for doing this for me."

"Of course," Taurin said.

"You should clean your house," Elle said helpfully.

Cynthia stared at her, affronted. "I did."

Elle raised an eyebrow, doubtful. Cynthia rolled her eyes and stomped off to the bathroom to change. She *had* cleaned the house, it just looked cluttered because it was tiny and she had a lot of things. And *yes,* she did need everything she owned. *No,* she wasn't going to get rid of anything.

Despite her fears, the dress fit exactly as it once had, perfectly hugging her curves, flattering to her chubby waist. She hesitated in front of the mirror for a moment, taking it all in, before deciding to let her hair stay loose and hang down around her shoulders. This was a good look, wasn't it? Tabitha would like it?

Shaking, she took in a long breath, relaxing her shoulders and forcing her fingers to stop trembling. Even if they did begin again a moment later. It would be okay. It didn't matter whether or not it went well; if it went well, that would be good, if it went poorly, she could handle it. There was nothing to worry about. Nothing to panic over.

Elle and Taurin were still there when she left the bathroom, doing her best to remain calm. Their eyes went wide at the sight of her, and Taurin gave a quiet, polite applause.

Elle simply shrugged. "I'd date you."

She shuffled, unable to meet their eyes. "So, uh . . ."

"We'll get out of your hair now," Taurin said, grabbing Elle by the back of the head and steering them toward the door.

"We just wanted to make sure you didn't back out of it," Elle finished with a grin. "You need to have fun."

Cynthia nodded, her fingers once again beginning to knot around each other. How could she have thought this was a good idea?

Taurin moved forward and squeezed her shoulder as he passed by. "Don't worry, you'll do great."

"Yeah." Elle clapped their hand onto Cynthia's back so forcefully she jumped. "Kiss her real good."

"Elle!" Cynthia choked out, face going hot. "What the hell!"

"Hey, that rhymes," they said with a laugh as they squeezed past to follow Taurin toward the door. The door slammed shut, leaving Cynthia alone.

Fear emerged in the silence.

This could go badly.

You'll have to move again.

She'll hate you.

You'll have to give it all up.

Ruphys hopped onto the back of the couch beside her. "You need to calm down."

Cynthia looked down sharply. "I am calm."

Ruphys made a noise, almost like he's beginning to cough up a hairball, which Cynthia had learned to interpret as close to a human scoff. "Could have fooled me."

Cynthia stared at him, bit her lip to try to keep it in, but it came charging out anyway. "What if this was a terrible idea?"

"Then you will eat lots of ice cream and cry over your weird films."

"No, but—"

"No, she isn't going to find out you're a witch and no, you won't have to move again even if she did," Ruphys said. "The situation is entirely different now."

"I know, but—"

"You're worried, I know," Ruphys said. "That's okay. But I am confident you will be okay."

"Okay. Oka—"

The doorbell rang.

"Fuck." Cynthia jumped, heartbeat slamming in her chest. "Fuck! I haven't even put on tea!"

"Well, go let her in first," Ruphys said quietly as he settled down onto a pillow.

"Right!" She hurried toward the door, patting her

damp palms off on the sides of her dress before reaching up and opening the door. Tabitha stood just outside, a vision in sunflower yellow, a nervous grin on her face. "Hi."

<h1 style="text-align:center">Chapter Eleven</h1>

"Hey," Tabitha breathed. Her brown hair bobbed in the wind, gentle curls blowing over her shoulder and into her face. She shifted and nudged the waves away, eyes darting back up to Cynthia. "So, are you going to let me in?"

"Oh!" Cynthia exclaimed. She swallowed hard, throat dry, and shifted to the side. One hand swept toward the crowded interior of her cabin. "Yes, of course, please come in!"

Tabitha stepped through the doorway into Cynthia's cottage, closing the door behind her before pausing to take it all in. Her eyes raked over the walls, over the tapestries and hangings, through the crowded little living area and a couch covered in pillows in blankets, Ruphys sitting on its back.

Growing in discomfort, Cynthia shifted as Tabitha remained quiet. What if she didn't like what she saw? What if, like Elle said, it looked dirty? What if—

"Your place is so cute!" Tabitha said, her voice high and light. "So homey and unique."

Unique. That was a good thing, right? "Thank you," Cynthia said, managing a smile. "I know it's small but—"

Tabitha burst out laughing. "Bigger than my apartment." She shakes her head, curls drifting loose over her shoulders, covering her face. Cynthia's fingers twitched to push the hair behind her ear.

"So, uh, you wanted tea?" Cynthia asked, shifting toward the kitchen before her fingers could win out and get what they wanted.

"I would love to have tea," Tabitha said, following her toward the kitchen.

Cynthia grabbed the kettle from the stove to fill up with water, glancing at the herbs around to figure out what she would serve Tabitha. What would she like? Lavender and hibiscus maybe?

"Woah." Cynthia paused, turning toward the doorway to find Tabitha frozen there, her eyes wide. They flicked around the ceiling, taking in the many bunches of dried herbs and flowers, as well as the braided cluster of garlic in the corner. "This is incredible." Her eyes finally landed on Cynthia. "Did you grow all this?"

Her lips pulled into a smile, cheeks warm. "Yeah," Cynthia said, looking around at her collection of herbs. She'd worked so hard on this, and it was truly impressive, if she did say so herself. "I have a green thumb."

She turned to set the kettle on the stove and turn it on, and when she turned around, Tabitha was right behind her.

"What tea are you making me?" she asked, leaning in to inspect the mugs on the counter—mugs Cynthia had forgotten to wash and put away.

"Uh, I'm not sure yet," Cynthia said, forced to swallow twice before she spoke. Tabitha was close.

"What's your favorite?" Tabitha asked. Her voice was low, sonorous, and Cynthia wanted to hear it more.

"Chamomile and lavender," Cynthia answered.

"Then I want that." Tabitha looked away—it took everything not to speak up to capture her attention once again—and reached up, brushing a bundle of lemon balm with her fingertip.

"What's this?"

"Lemon balm."

Tabitha shifted closer, reaching up to brush another bundle. A few bits of dried green leaves flaked off, landing on her yellow sweater. "And this?"

Cynthia swallowed hard, her mouth dry. Her fingers itched the brush the leaves from her sleeve. "Mint."

Tabitha leaned closer. She lifted herself up on her toes, tipping into Cynthia's space to reach the bundle hanging over her head. "And this?" she murmured, lips so close breath brushed Cynthia's cheek.

She couldn't help but rasp out the word, hardly able to breathe. "Lavender."

"Lavender," Tabitha repeated, the movement of her lips entrancing. Cynthia couldn't look away, even as heat grew between them.

Tabitha shifted closer.

Cynthia looked down, blinking her eyes away from Tabitha's lips, straining for air. Her gaze fell on the leaves sticking to Tabitha's sleeves and she couldn't resist. Her fingers reached out to brush them away, sparks flying up her hand when they touched.

"Sorry, you . . ." she looked back up, catching Tabitha's golden brown eyes for a single moment before she closed the distance.

Their lips brushed, and the heat was unbearable, burning under Cynthia's skin. She leaned in further, seeking relief in Tabitha's soft lips, lips sneaking between hers and tearing her apart.

Tabitha pulled her in, cupping her around the neck, fingers tangling in her hair. She tugged, and Cynthia moaned, melting into Tabitha as her knees went weak.

How could a person's lips taste so good?

Tabitha pushed into her, body hot and hard against her, electrifying to her core. Cynthia stumbled, one hand going to her waist—pulling her in harder, wishing she could be closer—the other fumbling for the counter behind her, desperate to remain upright.

Her fingers found the counter's edge as Tabitha pulled back just long enough to take a breath before dipping in again, first brushing her lips then falling into them, desperate and needy.

Cynthia braced against the counter, leg locking around Tabitha's, and bumped something. Glass rattled and tipped, and Cynthia pulled back to catch it just as it went over the edge—

And refused to strike the ground, bouncing back up into the air on an invisible string.

Chapter Twelve

All the breath left Cynthia's lungs, the heat leaving her body in a single gasp.

No.

The mug continued to hang there, sitting in the air as easily as it might on the counter.

This couldn't be happening.

Tabitha tried to pull her in again, hands tugging at her waist, but stopped when her tense body refused to move. She pulled back, frowning, following Cynthia's gaze.

Her mind raced, heart beating so fast it could burst, desperately trying to come up with a way to explain it. But how could she explain a mug hanging in mid air?

"Oh."

"I—I—" Words refused to form, refused to take shape, no explanation coming to her lips. She was screwed. There was no hiding that. This was a terrible idea and now she'd screwed everything up and she would have to move again and—

Tabitha bent over, snatching the mug out of the air and setting it on the counter. "That was a close one," she said, turning back to Cynthia with a smile.

Cynthia's mouth fell open.

"What?" Tabitha's eyebrows twisted together, eyes glinting. "Think I haven't seen a spell before?"

What?

She closed her mouth, opened to speak again, and the kettle whistled.

Cynthia broke away from Tabitha, hardly able to breath, quickly turning off the stove and removing the kettle from the stovetop. Everything shook. She wouldn't stop shaking.

"You okay?"

"You're a witch," Cynthia breathed.

Her lips pursed, the hint of a smile never leaving her eyes. "I thought you knew."

"I need to sit down."

She stumbled out of the kitchen, knees weak, grabbing for the couch. Tabitha was a witch. How could she be a witch? She'd been panicking for nothing. How did she not know?

Tabitha followed after her, biting her lip as she moved into the living room. She lowered onto the couch, sitting on the edge as if she didn't dare move closer to Cynthia.

"You're a witch," Cynthia said again, looking up at Tabitha. Tabitha nodded in confirmation.

"I really did think you knew," she said softly. "After I saw you talking with Nora, I thought she'd told you."

Cynthia shook her head, unable to repress a wild,

nervous laugh. "No. I had no idea."

"You've been panicking over that this whole time, haven't you?"

"Yeah," Cynthia said, not sure whether to laugh or cry. She'd been worried about nothing. For days, she'd been worried about nothing.

"I'm sorry," Tabitha said, reaching out to brush Cynthia's hand. "I really should have said something."

"It's okay," Cynthia breathed, twisting to look her in the face. She let out a breath, slumping toward Tabitha. "Now I don't have to worry."

"I told you," Ruphys said, speaking up from behind her on the couch. She jumped, twisting around to look at him.

"Did you know?"

He curled up primly, holding his head high. "I had my suspicions."

"You must be the familiar," Tabitha said, greeting Ruphys. "What's your name?"

"Ruphys. What's your familiar? Not a dog?"

"Yes, a dog," Tabitha said with a nod.

Ruphys stood up, walking away. "Cynthia, you cannot date her."

Cynthia twisted after him as he trotted toward the bedroom. "You don't get to make that call!"

She dropped back onto the couch and twisted toward Tabitha to find her grinning. "So dating is still an option?"

"What?" Cynthia asked.

"I was worried I'd scared you off," Tabitha admitted.

"*I* was worried I'd scared you off," Cynthia said, then laughed, unable to keep it down. "This is ridiculous."

"A tiny bit," Tabitha admitted.

"I'm going to kill Nora."

"I'll help," Tabitha said, then paused, a sneaky grin spreading across her face. "But only if you kiss me again."

A shiver ran down Cynthia's spine. "I like the sound of this deal—"

Tabitha cut her off with a kiss.

Chapter Thirteen

One Year Later

Cynthia bumped hips with Tabitha as she maneuvered around the kitchen, trying not to get in her way. The young teacher had a cup of tea in her hand and an assignment in the other, reading over a paper written in uneven, childish script.

When Tabitha sipped on the tea, Cynthia couldn't help but grin. She'd successfully converted Tabitha into a tea drinker, at least at home. The coffee maker she'd brought when she moved in last week still sat unused on the counter, surrounded by a pile of little pumpkins and gourds.

"Are you going to stay in here tonight?" she asked, setting the pot on the table. Hot pumpkin soup bubbled inside it, a new recipe Tabitha had suggested. She had a gift with food, Cynthia had discovered. The kitchen witch to Cynthia's green thumb.

"I'm not sure," Tabitha hummed, putting the paper down on the back of the couch, where it slid down to join the others in a pile. The cottage was a tiny bit overcrowded, they were still working on getting everything in working order. Tabitha insisted it *would* work, they just needed time, whenever Cynthia grew too anxious. "I have a lot of work to do."

"Well it's your own fault," Cynthia said, grinning at her to ensure she knew she was teasing. "You assigned it after all."

Tabitha swatted at her but grinned. "I do think I'll join you for a little while. I love Halloween here."

Cynthia sighed, leaning into Tabitha as the teacher came up behind her, wrapping her in a hug. "Me too."

Tabitha poked her in the side as she grinned. "I should make you dress up like I did last time."

"No!" Cynthia coughed, her face heating up. "No, I do not need that embarrassment again."

"Oh, but you make such a cute witch," Tabitha whined. She moved away, leaving Cynthia cold in the absence of her touch. "Maybe I'll just make you do it another time."

Cynthia shivered as the threat went straight to her core.

Tabitha sat down at the table across from her, peaking toward the bedroom, then leaned forward conspiratorially. "Not to jinx it, but I think Ruphys and Calliope are finally getting along."

Cynthia leaned back in her chair, trying to see through the door. "Really?"

Ruphys wasn't a fan of Tabitha's familiar, an Australian Shepherd with a personality that could only be described as joyful. Calliope desperately wanted to be friends with Ruphys, and the cat did not. But if they were finally getting along . . .

Finally far enough back, Cynthia managed to peek through the door and catch sight of them, then grinned. Ruphys lay in the middle of the bed, curled up with all fours beneath him, and Calliope lay around him, her tail beating happily against the quilt cover.

Cynthia sat back down, grinning. So they'd finally decided to get along.

"That took long enough," she said. It was one of the biggest reasons they'd held off for so long on moving in together; Ruphys was so difficult when it came to dogs. Luckily, Calliope was a persistent cuddlebug, and had apparently won him over.

"I told you this would work," Tabitha said, reaching across the table to give Cynthia's hand a squeeze.

"You did," she acknowledged.

"Which means I'm right, so you should kiss me."

She raised an eyebrow. "Are those the rules now?"

"Mhmm, yes."

"I think I can work with that," Cynthia said, grinning as she leaned over to give Tabitha a kiss. She couldn't help it, and she couldn't complain. Tabitha was the best thing that had ever happened to her, and she couldn't be happier.

The End.

Meet The Familiars

A Short Story

"Are you sure this is a good idea?" Cynthia asked over the phone, her voice shaking slightly. Partially because she was whispering, trying to avoid Ruphys's attention despite the fact that he was inside and she was not and he shouldn't have been able to hear her, partially out of anxiety.

"I'm sure," Tabitha said, her voice warm and soothing like always. Like tea. Cynthia could really use a cup of tea right now.

"He's not going to like it," Cynthia said, beginning to pace. Ruphys would be picking up on her anxiety by now, but she couldn't help it. This was a bad idea. Definitely a bad idea.

"They need to meet eventually, don't they?" Tabitha asked. "If we're going to be together, our lives are going to combine, at least on some level. And these are two very important parts of our lives, right?"

"Right," Cynthia murmured.

"So they have to meet. But it'll be okay. They love us, so it'll be okay."

"Okay," Cynthia breathed.

"Okay?"

"Okay."

Cynthia was still outside when Tabitha's car began crunching up the gravel driveway, only since the call ended, she'd begun pacing. And she couldn't stop.

This wouldn't go well.

Ruphys didn't like dogs. He'd made that expressly clear, again and again, and still wasn't happy that Tabitha's familiar was a dog. He'd accepted Tabitha despite the fact, which was a miracle in and of itself, but trying to introduce them to her dog?

It was a terrible idea.

Unfortunately, though, Tabitha was right. Their familiars were an inseparable part of their lives, pieces of their souls, of their magic, and they couldn't just get rid of them or ignore them. It wasn't possible, and Cynthia couldn't imagine a life without Ruphys, and was sure Tabitha couldn't imagine a life without Calliope. And Cynthia was beginning to realize she couldn't imagine a life without Tabitha either, which meant these parts of them had to meet.

None of those things mattered when Cynthia's anxiety flared. None of them affected the rising, irrational fear that this would—finally—be the time everything fell apart.

A force of fur slammed into her, nearly taking her knees out from beneath her. Calliope yelped with excitement, jumping up on Cynthia as she struggled to maintain her footing, the dog's attack only making it harder to breathe as the impact of paws on her chest took the air from her lungs.

"Hi, Calliope," Cynthia managed, taking the dog's paws and pushing her back. The red and white Australian Shepherd continued to dance around and wag her tail frantically, as if seeing Cynthia was the most exciting thing and hadn't just seen her yesterday.

"Hi, Cynthia!" the dog exclaimed, her voice high and punchy, as excited as the rest of her. "I'm so, so, so excited to see your farm! Tabitha talks about it all the time."

"Not all the time," Tabitha said, looking a bit bashful as she strode up beside Cynthia. An arm snaked around her waist, pulling her in so she was nestled against Tabitha's shoulder.

Cynthia opened her mouth to induct them into her home when Tabitha shocked her by cutting her off. "Why don't you go look around a bit, Calliope? Just don't get into any trouble."

"Oh! *Oh!* Of course not! That sounds exciting!" The dog was already running, taking off across the farm, probably to go destroy the first spring shoots of corn or whatever. Cynthia couldn't bring herself to call the dog back.

"Why-why did you do that?" Cynthia managed, wincing at how weak her voice sounded. It wouldn't come out right, caught behind short breaths and a heart that wouldn't stop its frantic beating.

Keeping her arm tight around Cynthia's waist, Tabitha shifted so they were face to face, giving Cynthia a full view of the concern written across her face. "Because you're shaking, baby," Tabitha murmured. "What's wrong?"

"Sorry," Cynthia said with a wince.

"No." Tabitha shook her head, lifting one hand to caress the side of Cynthia's face, guiding Cynthia to look her in the eye again. "No, you're not allowed to be sorry. Just tell me what's wrong."

"It's stupid." The words came out bitter from behind Cynthia's clenched teeth. Why was she like this? Why did she freak out over simple, mundane—magically mundane, at least—things.

"Okay, maybe? But what does it matter?" Tabitha demanded. "It's making you anxious, and don't try to deny that. So tell me, baby. Let me help."

She was pleading, and Cynthia hated it, but also, it softened her.

"It's this," she admitted, nodding toward where Calliope was yelping excitedly over . . . something. Cynthia didn't even care. "Introducing Ruphys and Calliope. What-what if it goes terribly?" It all came spilling out. "What if our familiars just can't get along and it ruins everything between us? What if—"

"No." Tabitha took her and kissed her forehead, cutting Cynthia off as she floundered over a whole new sensation. This comfort from Tabitha was like nothing she'd experienced before, and she didn't mind it. "No, baby, that's not going to happen. I don't know what we'll have to do or how long we'll have to take, but we'll figure this out." She took Cynthia's hands and entwined their fingers together. "We have all the time in the world."

Relief flooded through her and she sagged against Tabitha, letting herself get lost in the feeling of Tabitha's hand stroking the back of her head and their fingers locked together until she stopped shaking.

When she could breathe normally again, she lifted her head, glad to see a small grin split her girlfriend's lips. "You ready?"

"I am." Cynthia nodded.

"Want to go give Ruphys a heads up? I'll get Calliope and see if I can calm her down."

"Good idea," Cynthia said. She started toward the small cabin, trying to ignore the fears that flared once more. Tabitha was right, it would all be okay.

She stepped through the front door, only mildly surprised to find that Ruphys was not where she'd left him. He rarely stuck in one place for very long, unless it was a sun puddle on the floor.

"Ruphys?" She was barely able to bring herself to speak.

While most of her decor was black, it was easy enough to tell he wasn't in the living room, and he wasn't in the kitchen either when she poked her head in there. That left one last place, so she plodded through the house toward her bedroom.

Ruphys lifted his head slowly when she stepped through the bedroom door, and let out a deep, ragged sigh.

Then he stood up, uncurling from his ball on her pillows.

"Let's get this over with."

A groan escaped Cynthia's mouth. "You know?"

"You've been having an anxiety attack for an hour," Ruphys said dryly. "I know. Come on, take me to go meet this . . . *dog.*"

Cynthia opened up her arms and let Ruphys jump into them, holding him close to her chest as she made her way back out of the cabin. A sliver of hope wormed its way up through her heart at the sight of Tabitha and Calliope making their way toward her and Ruphys going willingly, albeit reluctantly.

Maybe this would take a while, but they could be a family, couldn't they?

Looking into Tabitha's shining brown eyes, Cynthia couldn't imagine anything else.

Acknowledgements

There are a number of people I need to thank but first, of course, is you, dear reader. Without you, this book would be purposeless. I'm glad I got a chance to share Cynthia and Tabitha and the rest of my lovely characters with you.

And of course, I need to thank Titta. Your feedback helped this book become the best version of itself, and is something I consider invaluable.

I also need to thank EJ. Your encouragement keeps me from quitting. I don't know what I'd do without you.

About The Author

Sapphire Lesbos is a nonbinary lesbian who grew up alone in the world, unseen and unheard, who wants to show people that being themself is an amazing thing, and that no one should be unable to love who they want. They currently live in the closet, working on the next edition to the Sapphire Lesbos world.

You can follow them on Instagram (@sapphire.lesbos) for updates, excerpts, and teasers for future projects.

Other works by Sapphire Lesbos:

Coffee Spies
A Summer To Live For